H. A. REY

Curious George

Learns the Alphabet

HOUGHTON MIFFLIN COMPANY BOSTON

Other Books About Curious George by H. A. Rey:

Printed in China

LEO   10 9 8 7 6 5 4 3 2 1

4500338239

This is George.

He lived with his friend, the man with the yellow hat. He was a good little monkey, but he was always curious.

This morning George was looking at some of his friend's books. They were full of little black marks and dots and lines, and George was curious: what could one do with them?

The man with the yellow hat came just in time.

"You don't tear a book apart to find out what's in it,"
he said. "You READ it, George. Books are full of stories.
Stories are made of words, and words are made of letters. If you want to read a story you first have to know
the letters of the alphabet. Let me show you."

The man took a big pad and began to draw.
George was curious.
"This is an A," the man said. "The A is the first
letter of the alphabet."

Now we add four feet and a long tail—
and the A becomes an ALLIGATOR
with his mouth wide open.
The word ALLIGATOR starts with an A.
This is a big A. There is also a small a.
All letters come in big and in small.

This is a small

It looks like a piece of an apple.

George knew alligators and apples.
You could eat apples. Alligators could
eat you if you didn't watch out.

7

This is a big **B**

The big B looks like a BIRD if we put feet on it and
a tail and a BILL. The word BIRD begins with a B.
BIRDS come in all colors. This BIRD is BLUE.
George loved to watch BIRDS.

This is a small

It could be a bee.

This bee is busy buzzing around a blossom.
The bee's body has black and yellow stripes.
George kept away from bees.
They might sting, and that would be bad.

This is a big **C**

We will make it into a CRAB—
a big CRAB,
with a shell, and feet, and two CLAWS.

This is a small

The small c is like the big C, only smaller,

so it becomes a small crab. It's cute.

Crabs live in the ocean.

They can swim or run sidewise and backwards.

Crabs can be funny, but they can also pinch you.

"You now have three
letters, George," the man said,
"A and B and C. With these three letters
you can make a WORD, the first word

you can read yourself. The word is

CAB

cab

You know what a cab is. I once took you for a ride in a cab, remember? And now let's draw the next letter."

The big **D**
could be a DINOSAUR.

There are no live DINOSAURS TODAY,
they have DIED out.
Those you see in museums are DUMMIES.
George had seen DINOSAURS in a museum once.

The small **d**
looks like a dromedary.

A dromedary is a camel with one hump.
Riding on a dromedary can make you dizzy because
it goes up and down—up and down—up and down.

desert

The big

is an ELEPHANT.
He is eating his EVENING meal: EGGPLANTS.
George loved ELEPHANTS.

The small e

could be the ear of a man,

or the ear of a monkey.
People's ears and monkeys' ears
look very much alike.

The big **F**

is a FIREMAN FIGHTING a FIRE.
Never FOOL the FIRE DEPARTMENT,
or you go to jail, and that's no FUN.

The small **f**

is a flower.
George's friend was fond of flowers.
George preferred food.

The big G

is a GOOSE.

GOOSE starts with a G, like GEORGE

The small **g**

is a goldfish.

He is in a glass bowl and looks giddy.

"Now you know seven letters, George," said the man, "A, B, C, D, E, F, G. With these letters we can already make quite a few words. I have written some of them down: you read them while I get you your lunch."

   "It seems the only
word you can read is BAD," said the man when he
came back. "I think we had enough for one morning. I'll feed you now and then you take your nap.
After your nap we'll go on with our letters."

The big **H**

is a HOUSE.

It stands on a HILL behind a HEDGE.

George's HOME used to be the jungle.

Now he lives in a HOUSE.

The small **h**

is a horse.

He is happy because he has heaps of hay.

George had his own horse—a hobby horse.

The big 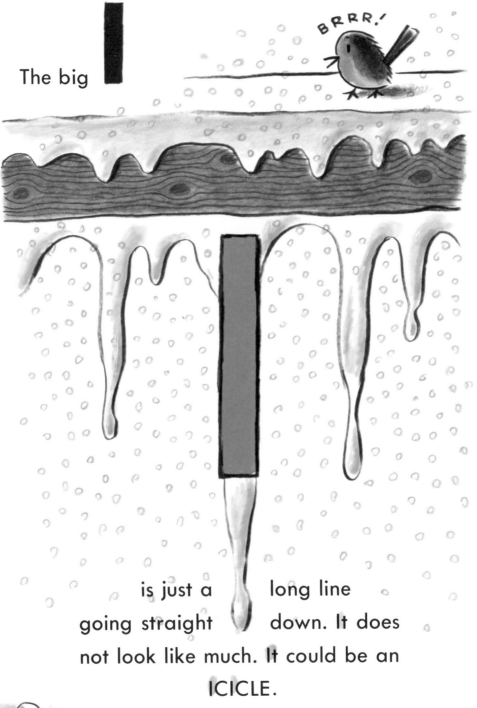 is just a long line going straight down. It does not look like much. It could be an ICICLE.

The small **i** is a line with a dot on top.
It could be an iguana.

An iguana is a sort of lizard.
Iguanas don't like ice. They like the warm sunshine.
So does George.

The big **J**
is a JAGUAR.

JAGUARS live in the JUNGLE.
George knew JAGUARS.
He had lived in the JUNGLE once.

The small **j**

is a jack-in-the-box.
George had a jack-in-the-box as a toy.
He just loved to make it jump.

The big **K**

is a big KANGAROO called KATY.

The small **k**

is a small kangaroo.

He is Katy's kid.

The big **L**

is a LION.
He is LUCKY. He is going to have
LEG of LAMB for LUNCH, and he LOVES it.

The small

is a lean lady.
She is strolling along a lake licking a lollipop.
George liked lollipops.

The big **M**

is a MAILMAN.

His name is MISTER MILLER. He brings a letter.

Maybe it's for ME, thinks George.

The small **m**

is a mouse.
He is munching mints.

"And do you know what else it is?" said
the man to George: "M is the thirteenth letter
of the A B C. The whole alphabet has only

26 letters, so thirteen is just half of it. You can make lots of words with these letters. Why don't you try? Here's a pad and pencil."

George started to think of words, and then he wrote them down. It was fun to make words out of letters.

"Let me see," said the man. "Ball – Milk – Cake – Ham – Jam – Egg – Lime – Feed – Kid – that's very good.

But what on earth is a Dalg or a Glidj or a Blimlimlim? There are no such things. Just ANY letters do not make words, George.

Well, let's look at some new letters now."

The big **N**

is a NAPKIN

standing on a dinner plate. It looks NEAT.
George had seen NAPKINS folded that way
in the restaurant when he was a dishwasher.

The small **n**

is a nose
in the face of a man.
He has a new blue necktie on
and is nibbling noodles.

The big  is a big OSTRICH,

and the small

is a small ostrich, of course.

Ostriches eat odd objects.
One ostrich once had tried to eat a bugle
that belonged to George.

The big **P**

is a big PENGUIN,

and the small **p** is a small penguin.

These penguins live near the South Pole.
They use their flappers as paddles.
George knew penguins from the Zoo.

PLOP!

The big **Q**

is a QUAIL.

QUAILS have short tails.

You must keep QUIET if you want to

watch QUAILS. They are quite shy.

The small  is a quarterback.

A quarterback has to be quick. George was quick. He would qualify for quarterback.

"And now get your football, George," said the man, "it will do you good to play a little before we go on with your letters."

George knew how to play
the game. He knew how to
carry the ball,

and how to
take a three-
point stance,

and how to get ready
for the kick-off.

He was a fine halfback, too,

and he could make a short pass,
or recover a fumble.

"Good game," said the man, "but
time's up now: back to the alphabet!"

The big **R**

is a RABBIT.

Some RABBITS are white with RED eyes.

RABBITS love RADISHES.

George loved RABBITS. He had one as a pet.

The small **r**

is a rooster.

The rooster crows when the sun rises.

Two roosters will start a rumpus.

They really can get rough.

The big

is a big SNAIL,

and the small **S**

is a small snail.
Snails are slow. They sneak into their shells
when they are scared of something.
George thought snails looked silly.

The big **T**

is a TABLE.
The TABLE is set for TWO. It is TIME for TEA.
George did not care for TEA,
but he liked TOAST.

The small ✝ is a tomahawk.

George had a toy tomahawk.
It was a tiny one.
He took it along when he played outside.

"Now it's time for a snack,"
said the man. "Run over to
the baker, George,

and hand him this note. Then come
right back with the doughnuts, one dozen of
them, and no tricks, please!"

George was curious. He looked at the note
the man had written. One dozen doughnuts . . .

Maybe he could write something on
it too? How about writing TEN
instead of ONE? He had just
learned the T . . . First a T—
then an E—then an N . . .

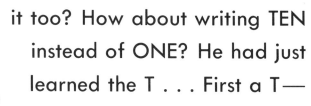

"Hmm," said the baker, "ten dozen doughnuts is quite a lot, but that's what the note says. We need an extra-big bag for them."

"Why, George!" cried the man.
Then he saw the note.
"Well, that comes from teaching
the alphabet to a little monkey.
And I told you: no tricks!"

TEN DOZEN
ONE DOZEN
DOUGH NUTS

"You may not eat any
doughnuts now, George.
Put them back in the bag
and let's go on with
the letters!"

The big **U**
is a big UMBRELLA
standing UPRIGHT.

The umbrella handle
is also
like a **u**.

George knew how to USE an UMBRELLA.

The small **U** is a small umbrella.

When it is raining umbrellas are useful
but you must keep under the umbrella
unless you want to get wet.
George thought rain was a nuisance.

The big **V**

For George
from the man
with the
yellow
hat

is a big **V**ALENTINE,

and the small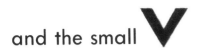

is a small valentine.

George loved valentines.

He got several valentine cards every year.

One card came from Nevada.

The big **W** and the small **W** are WHISKERS, big ones and small ones.

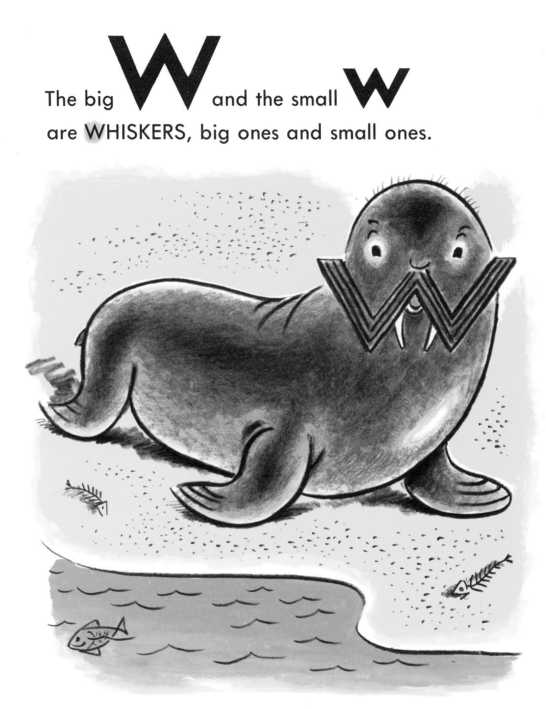

A WALRUS has WHISKERS.

Some men  have whiskers

and cats have whiskers.

George did not have whiskers
but he was curious how
he would look if he did.

The next letter of the alphabet is X.

The big **X** and the small **X**
look alike, only one is big and one is
small, just like the big W and the small w,
or the V, or the U, or the S, and some of
the other letters.

"BUT," said the  man, "there are
few words that start with an
X, and they don't look like an X—

except one, and that is
Xmas!"

Santa stands for Xmas.

There is only one Santa so we need only one picture.

George thought Xmas was exciting.

The big **Y**

is a big YAK

and the small **Y**

is a small yak: he is still young.
Yaks live in Tibet. If you haven't seen any yaks yet
you may find one at the zoo.

The big **Z**

is a big ZEBRA,

and the small **Z** is a small zebra.

The zebras are zipping along with zest.

"And do you know what?" said the man, "Z is the last letter. Now you know all the 26 letters of the alphabet—

and NOW you may have the doughnuts."